This
Buttons Family
book belongs to

Cherry and Charlie and Baby Lou,

We're the Buttons, we're just like you!

And every day there's something new

For Cherry and Charlie and Baby Lou!

First published 2012 by Walker Books Ltd
87 Vauxhall Walk, London SE11 5HJ

10 9 8 7 6 5 4 3 2 1

Text © 2012 Vivian French
Illustrations © 2012 Sue Heap

This book has been typeset in HVD Bodedo

Printed in China

British Library Cataloguing in
Publication Data: a catalogue record
for this book is available from
the British Library

ISBN 978-1-4063-2855-4

www.walker.co.uk

The Buttons Family
New Shoes

Vivian French

illustrated by
Sue Heap

WALKER BOOKS
AND SUBSIDIARIES
LONDON • BOSTON • SYDNEY • AUCKLAND

"My toes hurt," said Charlie.

"Hmm... It looks like you need new shoes," said Mum.

"My toes hurt too," said Cherry. "Hurtie toes!" said Baby Lou.

Mum sighed. "You ALL need new shoes. We'd better go shopping."

"Yes!" shouted Cherry.
"Ess!" shouted Baby Lou.

"I don't want new shoes,"
Charlie said.

"New shoes are
LOVELY,"
Mum told him.

At the shoe shop Cherry and Baby Lou went in, but Charlie stayed outside.

"I don't want new shoes," he said.

Mum smiled. "Why don't you just come and watch us?" "OK," said Charlie. "But I'm not doing any trying on."

Cherry chose shiny red shoes.

Baby Lou chose bright
yellow boots.

"I don't want new shoes," Charlie told the shop lady.

Charlie looked at his feet.
"My toes can't talk."
"But I can hear them," said
the shop lady.

"They're saying, 'Ouch! We're squashed! We can't grow straight.'"

Charlie took off his shoes. "What are they saying now?"

"They're saying, 'WOW, that's better! Now we've got some space!'"

"Oh." Charlie
wriggled his toes.

"What happens if toes are squashed?"
"They grow crooked, and they hurt," said the shop lady. "And they can get lumps and bumps and blisters. Would your toes like to try a little more space, do you think?"
Charlie nodded.

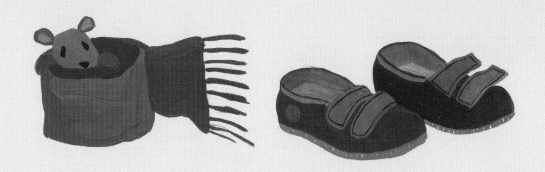

Charlie tried on shiny shoes ...

lace-up shoes ...

red trainers ...

green trainers ...

boots ...

and super racer trainers.

"Goodness," said Mum, "look at the time! Charlie, please make up your mind!" Charlie looked hurt. "I'm waiting for my toes to say which ones they like best."

The shop lady laughed. "They say you choose."
"I like these," Charlie picked the super racer trainers. "Good choice," said the shop lady. "Your toes'll be very happy in those."

Charlie jumped up and down
as Mum paid for their shoes.
Then Cherry, Charlie
and Baby Lou
jumped ...

ALL the way ...

... back home.

"There!" said Mum. "That wasn't so bad, was it?"

"I love my shoes," said Cherry. "Lovie shoes," said Baby Lou. "And I've just heard my toes talking," said Charlie. "They want to go shoe shopping again tomorrow!"

There are six **Buttons Family** books to collect.
Which ones have you read?

New Shoes

Charlie's shoes are too tight!
He says he doesn't want
new ones, but what do
his toes say?

ISBN 978-1-4063-2855-4

Going to
the Doctor

Cherry's got a nasty cold.
How will Mum persuade
her to go to the doctor?

ISBN 978-1-4063-2857-8

Staying with Gran

Cherry, Charlie and Baby Lou have
never stayed with Gran on their
own before. Will Gran make sure
they feel at home?

ISBN 978-1-4063-2860-8

First Day
at Playschool

It's Cherry's first day
at playschool and she's
feeling a little shy.
How will she settle in?

ISBN 978-1-4063-2856-1

The
Babysitter

Mum and Dad are going out.
What do Cherry, Charlie
and Baby Lou think of the
new babysitter?

ISBN 978-1-4063-2858-5

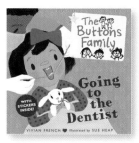

Going to
the Dentist

It's time for the Buttons
to go to the dentist!
How will they get on at
their check-up?

ISBN 978-1-4063-2859-2

Available from all good booksellers